Dear Parent:
Your child's love of readi...

Every child learns to read in a different ~~way~~... speed. Some go back and forth between favorite books again and again. Others read through each level in order. You can help your young reader improve and become more confident by encouraging his or her own interests and abilities. From books your child reads with you to the first books he or she reads alone, there are I Can Read Books for every stage of reading:

SHARED READING
Basic language, word repetition, and whimsical illustrations, ideal for sharing with your emergent reader

BEGINNING READING
Short sentences, familiar words, and simple concepts for children eager to read on their own

READING WITH HELP
Engaging stories, longer sentences, and language play for developing readers

READING ALONE
Complex plots, challenging vocabulary, and high-interest topics for the independent reader

ADVANCED READING
Short paragraphs, chapters, and exciting themes for the perfect bridge to chapter books

I Can Read Books have introduced children to the joy of reading since 1957. Featuring award-winning authors and illustrators and a fabulous cast of beloved characters, I Can Read Books set the standard for beginning readers.

A lifetime of discovery begins with the magical words **"I Can Read!"**

Visit www.icanread.com for information
on enriching your child's reading experience.

Planet 51: Welcome to Planet 51 © 2009 Ilion Animation Studios, HandMade Films International & A3 Films. Planet 51™ and all related characters, places, names and other indicia are trademarks of Ilion Studios, S.L., HandMade Films International Limited & A3 Films S.L. All Rights Reserved. Printed in the United States of America. No part of this book may be used or reproduced in any manner whatsoever without written permission except in the case of brief quotations embodied in critical articles and reviews. For information address HarperCollins Children's Books, a division of HarperCollins Publishers, 10 East 53rd Street, New York, NY 10022. www.icanread.com

Library of Congress catalog card number: 2009930267
ISBN 978-0-06-184411-9
Typography by Rick Farley

09 10 11 12 13 LP/WOR 10 9 8 7 6 5 4 3 2 1 ❖   First Edition

I Can Read!

READING 2 WITH HELP

PLANET 51

WELCOME TO PLANET 51

Adapted by Gail Herman

HARPER

An Imprint of HarperCollinsPublishers

Far, far from Earth,
Planet 51 spins
slowly in space.

The people who live
on Planet 51 are green.
But they aren't that different
from people on Earth.
They watch movies,
go to school, and shop at stores.

Lem is a regular teenager.

He works at the planetarium.

Lem loves outer space.

"There are one thousand stars

out there!" Lem tells visitors.

"But only our planet has life on it."

That's what Lem has always learned,

and Lem believes what he is told.

But one day,

Lem's world is changed forever.

An astronaut has landed

on Planet 51.

"He must be an alien!" says Lem.

The astronaut's name is Chuck.
He wants to explore the planet,
then go right home.
He doesn't think that
he'll meet any aliens.
But Chuck is in
for a surprise.
On Planet 51,
Chuck is the alien!

"What can I do?" says Chuck.
"I'm just a good-looking guy
who's never had to work hard.
My spaceship even flies itself!"
he tells Lem.

Now Chuck must prove

that he has the right stuff,

or he may never return to Earth.

Lem's friend Skiff is ready to help.

Skiff knows all about aliens.

He works in a comic book store.

"That's how I know that aliens

will turn us into zombies!" he says.

Then Skiff meets Rover.

Rover is Chuck's robot.

"Awww! He's kind of cute!" says Skiff.

"Maybe aliens aren't all bad."

Rover is on Planet 51 to get rocks.

That's his job.

Rover likes to play fetch
even more than he likes rocks.

He and Skiff are made

for each other.

Eckle lives next door to Lem.

He'd rather watch alien movies

than do anything else.

His mom has to drag him away.

Eckle loves aliens!

Eckle can't believe that there is

a real alien right next door!

"Can I have your autograph?"

Eckle asks Chuck.

Neera is Eckle's sister.
She is smart and pretty,
and she wants to make
her planet a better place.

Lem wants to impress Neera.

But Neera thinks Lem

sticks to the rules too much.

"You have to think for yourself,"

she tells him.

Glar is Neera's friend.

Glar likes to protest

for what he thinks is right.

But Lem thinks Glar protests

just so he can get attention.

"You're bumming me out,"

Glar tells General Grawl

at a protest meeting.

General Grawl is the head of the army.

Grawl wants his planet to be safe.

"The battle against the aliens

has begun!" he tells his soldiers.

"Get Professor Kipple!"

Professor Kipple is an expert
on aliens.

"The alien is just like us,"
Kipple tells a soldier.

"Except that he can
take over your brain."

Grawl needs Kipple to come up
with a plan to save the planet.
"I'll take care of that alien
in no time!" says Kipple.

"Wait!" Lem says to General Grawl.

"You're not afraid of the alien.

You're afraid of the unknown.

But the unknown doesn't mean

the end of everything.

It can actually be the beginning."

General Grawl and

Professor Kipple

hear what Lem has to say.

They realize that maybe Chuck

isn't so different, after all.

When it's time for Chuck to leave,

Chuck and Lem hug.

"If you ever make it to Earth,

I'm in the phone book,"

Chuck tells him.

"Good-bye!" Chuck calls

to the general, the soldiers,

and all the others.

They wave as Chuck's ship takes off.

Planet 51 is quite a place.

Lem and Chuck

will never forget this time,

or each other.